Published in the United States of America

ISBN: 978-1-940927-18-3

Green Oak Press is an imprint of Quincentennial Publishing Co.

A LIGHT OMNI MEDIA PRODUCTION through MAJOR STAR PUBLISHING

www.majorstar.us

A MAJOR STAR PUBLISHING COMPANY

To Lily and Aidan - You can do anything you hope for.

To Justin - For your constant love and support.

To Dad, Mom, Aunt Marie, and Dr. Teri - For believing in me.

To all Lily's Hope Families - Keep holding onto hope.

- JMD

To my husband, Dan - For your loving and unconditional support.

To my children, Daniel and Alexander - For your energy and laughter.

And to my loving parents - For your guidance.

- HLC

Lily's Hope

A Preemie's Journey of Hope

Jennifer M. Driscoll and Lilian Hope Driscoll
Illustrated by Heather L. Corey

My name is Lilian Hope.
This story is about hope
and what it means to my family.
Do you know what hope means?

Hope means

wishing for good things to happen.

My parents were filled with hope when they found out
they were going to be a mommy and a daddy.
The doctor told them I would be born in September.

I surprised my parents and was born two months early.
Because I was born prematurely,
I was sick and spent a long time in the hospital.

My parents' hope gave me strength to get well.

My doctors and nurses took good care of me
at the hospital.
They hoped I would get better quickly.

After a few weeks, I started to feel better.
I got stronger because everyone
hoped and believed in me.

My doctors said I could leave the hospital
with my mommy and daddy.

Hope traveled with us on our journey home.

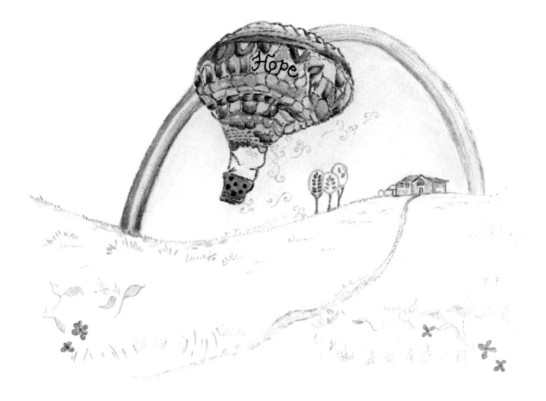

Hope followed me to my many doctor appointments
during the next five years.

As I got stronger and healthier,

hope grew with me.

When I was five years old,
I found out that I was going to be a big sister.
I was filled with hope for my new best friend.

My little brother, Aidan, was also born early.
I hoped he would be healthy and come home quickly.

Aidan saw doctors after he came home, just as I did.
Hope was with us every step of the way.

My family believed in hope so much that
they wanted to help families like us.
We started the Lily's Hope Foundation.

Lily's Hope Foundation provides aid and hope
to families with babies like Aidan and me.
Now, we share hope with every family we help.

Aidan and I are proof that there is hope in all difficult situations, especially for babies who are born early. We hope families with premature babies know there are people reaching out to them to provide aid and hope.

Meet the Authors

Jennifer Driscoll and her husband, Justin, had two children born prematurely: Lilian Hope and Aidan Patrick. Jennifer and Justin know first-hand what the families of Lily's Hope Foundation experience. After these experiences with their children, they were inspired to create Lily's Hope Foundation to help other parents of premature babies during this challenging time in their lives. Aside from being Co-Founder and Executive Director of Lily's Hope Foundation, Jennifer works full time for an engineering firm in Allentown, PA. Jennifer graduated with her Bachelor's Degree in 2005 and her Master's in Business Administration in 2011, both from Moravian College, in Bethlehem, PA. Jennifer and her daughter, Lilian Hope, co-wrote *Lily's Hope*.

Meet the Illustrator

Heather Leigh Corey brings a style that is both lyrical and whimsical. Her artistic background includes sculpture, art education, and illustration. She received her BA from Moravian College and MFA from The Pennsylvania Academy of the Fine Arts. Heather lives in Glen Rock, New Jersey, with her husband and two sons; she also enjoys running, interior design, and photography.

Lily's Hope Foundation

The Lily's Hope Foundation is a 501(c)(3) non-profit organization that empowers families with urgent and unexpected needs due to premature birth. Lily's Hope Foundation accomplishes this by providing resources, aid, and hope to families with preemies through our Packages of Hope program. We support our NICU families by providing them with essential items since they have been unable to prepare for their child's early arrival. Our Lily's Hope Foundation Families that are in the middle of this medical crisis are referred to us by hospital case workers, hospital staff, and word of mouth. We work with each individual family to answer their specific needs by way of our Packages of Hope. Our Packages of Hope include items that can often be expensive and difficult to find. Examples of the care package contents are micro-preemie/preemie clothing, preemie diapers, car seats or car seat beds, bassinets, gift cards for use toward transportation to the NICU, and more.

Lily's Hope® and Lily's Loop® are registered trademarks with the United States Patent and Trademark Office. For more information, please visit our website at www.LilysHopeFoundation.org.

51754613R00018

Made in the USA
Middletown, DE
15 November 2017